Dear Parent:

Congratulations! Your child is taking the first steps on an exciting journey. The destination? Independent reading!

STEP INTO READING® will help your child get there. The program offers five steps to reading success. Each step includes fun stories and colorful art. There are also Step into Reading Sticker Books, Step into Reading Math Readers, Step into Reading Phonics Readers, Step into Reading Write-In Readers, and Step into Reading Phonics Boxed Sets—a complete literacy program with something to interest every child.

Learning to Read, Step by Step!

Ready to Read Preschool–Kindergarten
• big type and easy words • rhyme and rhythm • picture clues
For children who know the alphabet and are eager to begin reading.

Reading with Help Preschool–Grade 1
• basic vocabulary • short sentences • simple stories
For children who recognize familiar words and sound out new words with help.

Reading on Your Own Grades 1–3
• engaging characters • easy-to-follow plots • popular topics
For children who are ready to read on their own.

Reading Paragraphs Grades 2–3
• challenging vocabulary • short paragraphs • exciting stories
For newly independent readers who read simple sentences with confidence.

Ready for Chapters Grades 2–4
• chapters • longer paragraphs • full-color art
For children who want to take the plunge into chapter books but still like colorful pictures.

STEP INTO READING® is designed to give every child a successful reading experience. The grade levels are only guides. Children can progress through the steps at their own speed, developing confidence in their reading, no matter what their grade.

Remember, a lifetime love of reading starts with a

For Emma —R.H.

Step into Reading, Random House, and the Random House colophon are registered trademarks of Random House, Inc.

Visit us on the Web!
StepIntoReading.com
randomhouse.com/kids

Educators and librarians, for a variety of teaching tools, visit us at
randomhouse.com/teachers

ISBN 978-0-7364-2908-5 (trade) — ISBN 978-0-7364-8106-9 (lib. bdg.)
Printed in the United States of America
10 9 8 7 6 5 4 3 2

Jewels for a Princess

By Ruth Homberg

Illustrated by Studio IBOIX, Andrea Cagol,
Gabriella Matta, Cristina Spagnoli, Valeria Turati,
and the Disney Storybook Artists

Random House 🏠 New York

The Prince
gives Cinderella
a sparkly blue ring.
She loves it!

Cinderella shows
her new ring
to her friends.

Gus wants a ring,

too.

He finds

something shiny.

It is just a marble.

Cinderella shares
her ring with Gus.
He puts it
on his tail!

Cinderella loves
her friends.
They are
the best gift!

Jasmine finds
a fancy jewel.
Whose is it?

A guard gives Jasmine
the purple jewel.
It is a surprise
from Aladdin!

Jasmine puts the jewel
in her hair.
It sparkles and shines.

Aladdin and Abu
take Jasmine
on a magic carpet ride.
She loves
her new jewel.

Jasmine loves
Aladdin and Abu
most of all.

Aurora gets
a new crown.
It has a lovely
pink jewel.

Aurora is
a pretty princess!
A painter paints
her picture.

The Good Fairies
wave their wands.
The jewel shines!

Aurora thanks
her family and friends
for the crown.
She is so happy!

Ariel swims and plays
with her friends.

They find
many jewels.
Flounder shares them
with Ariel.

King Triton
makes a jewel necklace.
He puts the necklace
around Ariel's neck.

The jewel
reminds Ariel
of her friends
in the sea.

Rapunzel wears
a tiara that glitters.

It has red, white,
and green jewels.

Flynn thinks Rapunzel
is a perfect princess!

Tiana and Naveen go
to the bayou.
Naveen gives Tiana
a special stone.

Tiana thanks Naveen.
She gives him
a big hug.

Mama Odie makes
the stone shimmer.
It is
the perfect gift.

Tiana loves
her new jewel.
She wears it
to a party.

She thanks Mama Odie
and Naveen.

Tiana's friends are
the best jewels of all!